This

🐾 Mucky Pup Adventure 🐾

belongs to:

_____

For Janice

First published in Great Britain in 1998 by Andersen Press Ltd., 20 Vauxhall Bridge Road, London SW1V 2SA.

This paperback edition first published in 2007 by Andersen Press Ltd.

Published in Australia by Random House Australia Pty., Level 3, 100 Pacific Highway, North Sydney, NSW 2060.

Copyright © Ken Brown, 1998

The rights of Ken Brown to be identified as the author and illustrator

of this work have been asserted by him in accordance with the Copyright, Designs and Patents Act, 1988.

All rights reserved. Colour separated in Switzerland by Photolitho AG, Zürich.

Printed and bound in Singapore.

10 9 8 7 6 5 4 3 2 1

British Library Cataloguing in Publication Data available.

ISBN 978 1 84270 653 4

This book has been printed on acid-free paper

Mucky Pup's Christmas

Written and illustrated by

Ken Brown

Andersen Press
London

Mucky Pup was busy being helpful.
He collected the post, sampled the cake,

and rearranged the tree. Clever Mucky Pup!

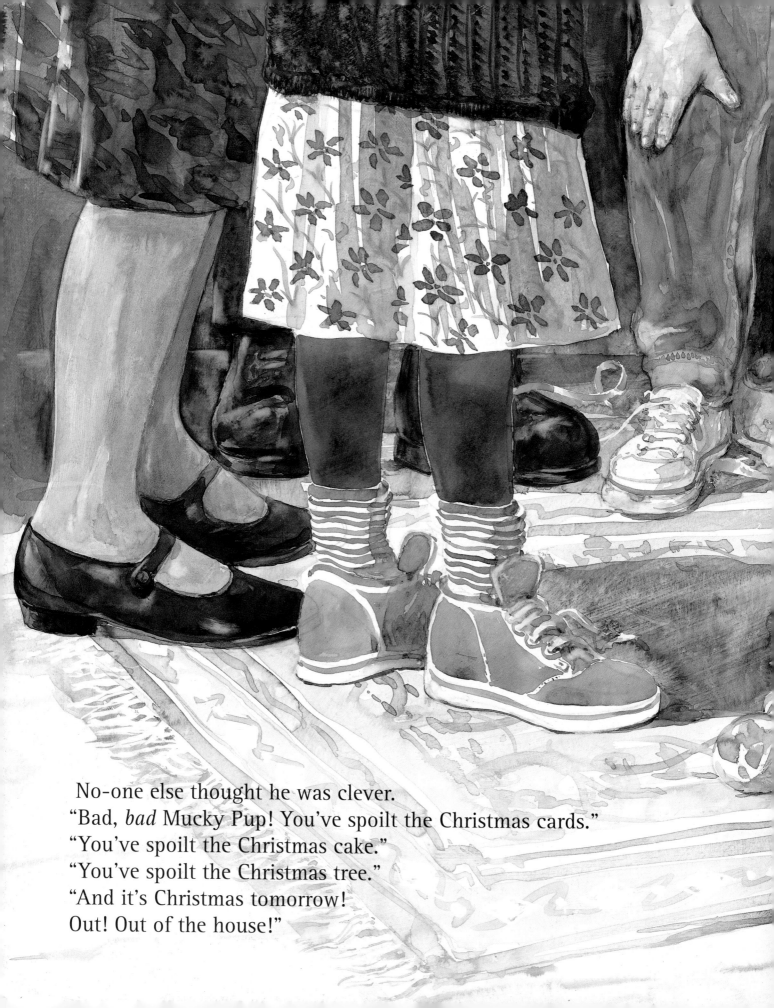

No-one else thought he was clever.
"Bad, *bad* Mucky Pup! You've spoilt the Christmas cards."
"You've spoilt the Christmas cake."
"You've spoilt the Christmas tree."
"And it's Christmas tomorrow!
Out! Out of the house!"

Mucky Pup went to find Pig.
"What's up?" said Pig.
"They don't want me," said
Mucky Pup miserably.
"They say I've spoilt this
Christmas thing. Do you
know what it is, Pig?"

Pig didn't know.
Nor did Horse or Hen or Duck.
Cat *said* she knew but wasn't telling.
"It doesn't sound much fun whatever it is," said Pig.
"Cheer up, Mucky Pup. Stay here with us tonight."

So Mucky Pup snuggled down in the soft, warm straw with Pig.
He thought he could hear someone calling his name,
but perhaps it was just a dream.

The next
morning,
everything was clean
and white and new.
"Do you think it's the Christmas
thing, Pig?" asked Mucky Pup.
"Can't be," said Pig. "It looks too much fun.
Come on, Mucky Pup. Let's play!"

And that's what they did . . .

They skated,

they snowballed,

they sledged and . . .

Wheeeeeeeeeeeeeeeeeeeeeeeeeee...

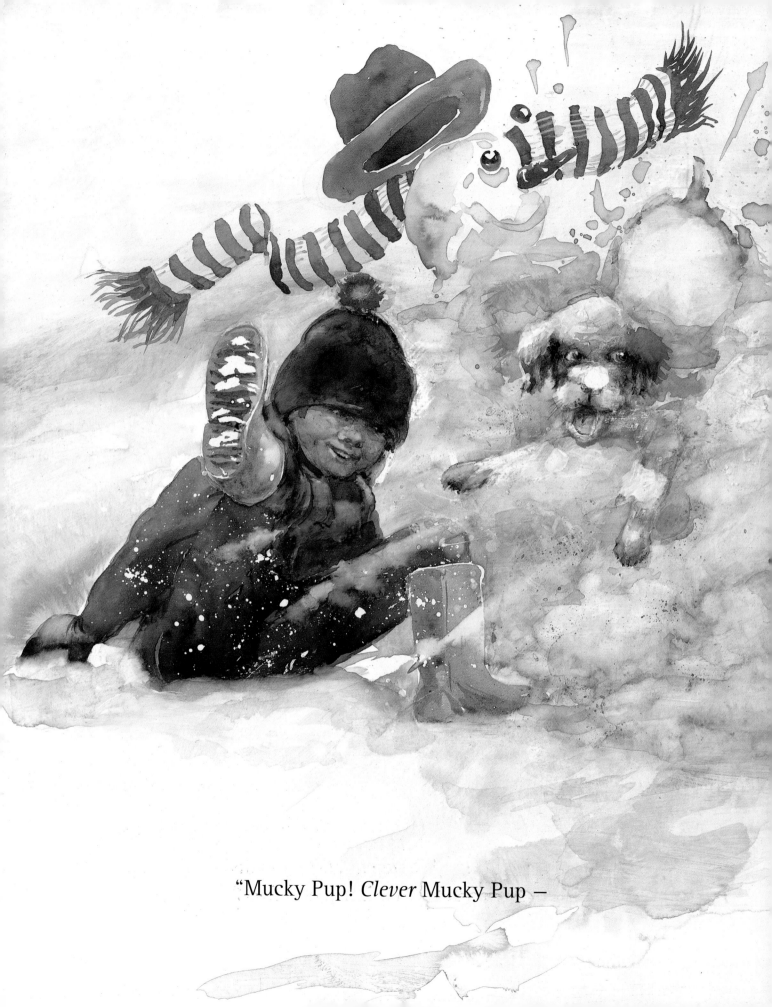

"Mucky Pup! *Clever* Mucky Pup –

you found us! We've called and called.
Don't you know? It's Christmas Day!"

And they put him on the sled and went back to
the warm, bright house, where Mucky Pup
at last found out what Christmas was.
There were parcels, and paper,
and his very own present . . .

. . . and it was *lots* of fun.

"I didn't spoil Christmas after all,"
thought Mucky Pup happily.
"I shall tell Pig tomorrow!"

Look out for more

🐾 Mucky Pup Adventures 🐾

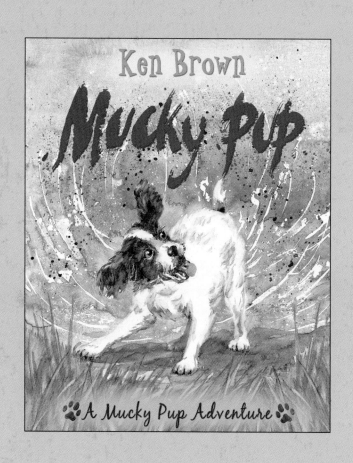